The Dahlmanac

An almanac is a month-by-month book of facts and information. Roald Dahl liked to collect odd facts. So, *The Dahlmanac* is a unique mixture of the two.

It's a trip through a year, with letters and observations by Roald Dahl himself about everything under the sun: why he hated Christmas, what he got up to as a boy and what's the best time of the year for conkers. Plus, there are lots of weird and wonderful facts inspired by Roald Dahl – how people used to test for witches, the story behind the Gunpowder Plot and how the Aztecs drank chocolate – along with some jokes, quizzes and the odd scrumdiddlyumptious recipe thrown in for good measure.

Roald Dahl inspired *The Dahlmanac*, and it's exactly the sort of book he would have loved to read.

Discover the Gloriumptious World of Roald Dahl

Also available on Puffin Audio

THE Dahlmanac

A year with ROALD DAHL

fun facts and jokes

with illustrations by QUENTIN BLAKE
compiled by KAY WOODWARD

PUFFIN

PUFFIN BOOKS

Published by the Penguin Group
Penguin Books Ltd, 80 Strand, London WC2R 0RL, England
Penguin Group (USA) Inc., 375 Hudson Street, New York, New York 10014, USA
Penguin Group (Canada), 90 Eglinton Avenue East, Suite 700, Toronto, Ontario, Canada M4P 2Y3
(a division of Pearson Penguin Canada Inc.)
Penguin Ireland, 25 St Stephen's Green, Dublin 2, Ireland (a division of Penguin Books Ltd)
Penguin Group (Australia), 250 Camberwell Road, Camberwell, Victoria 3124, Australia
(a division of Pearson Australia Group Pty Ltd)
Penguin Books India Pvt Ltd, 11 Community Centre, Panchsheel Park, New Delhi – 110 017, India
Penguin Group (NZ), 67 Apollo Drive, Mairangi Bay, Auckland 1310, New Zealand
(a division of Pearson New Zealand Ltd)
Penguin Books (South Africa) (Pty) Ltd, 24 Sturdee Avenue, Rosebank, Johannesburg 2196, South Africa

Penguin Books Ltd, Registered Offices: 80 Strand, London WC2R 0RL, England

penguin.com

First published 2006
1

Made and printed in England by Clays Ltd, St Ives plc

British Library Cataloguing in Publication Data
A CIP catalogue record for this book is available from the British Library

ISBN-13: 978–0–141–32189–9
ISBN-10: 0–141–32189–X

September

Roald Dahl went to boardiing school when he was nine. He wrote to his mother once a week without fail, and she kept all his letters! As you can see, young Roald's spelling was awful.

Dear Mama

I am sorry I have not writting before. I hope none of you have got coalds. IT is qaite a nice day To-day, I am just going To church. I hope (mike) is quite all right now, and (buzz) Major Cottam is going To recite some Thing caled ("as you like it") To night. plese could you send me some (conkers) as quick as you can, but don't dont send To meny, the just send them in a Tin and wrap it up in paper

Love from

BOY

Probabl Dahl family pets

A play by Shakespear

See page 12

Young Roald sometimes signed his letters like this.

1

Happy birthday, Roald!

**Roald Dahl was born on
13 September 1916.**
Other famous people born
the same month include:

☆ Beyoncé Knowles (singer and actor)
   4 September 1981

☆ Queen Elizabeth I (the famous Tudor queen)
   7 September 1533

☆ Prince Harry (royal prince)
   15 September 1984

☆ Agatha Christie (deadly crime author)
   15 September 1890

☆ George Cadbury (real chocolate-factory owner)
   19 September 1890

☆ T.S. Eliot (poet)
   26 September 1888

☆ Serena Williams (whizzy tennis player)
   26 September 1981

☆ Gwyneth Paltrow (actor)
   29 September 1972

Did you know?

13 September is the 256th day of the year, apart from leap years, when it's the 257th day.

True or false?

Every year, Roald Dahl had an enormous, gooey, squidgy, sticky chocolate sponge cake for his birthday – just like the one that Bruce Bogtrotter ate in *Matilda*.

False

Although Roald loved chocolate, he was not fond of chocolate-flavoured food – including chocolate cake.

How to Say 'Happy birthday' in 11 different languages

Hartelijk gefeliciteerd!
Dutch

Joyeux anniversaire!
French

Janam din ki badhai!
Hindi

Hau`oli la hanau!
Hawaiian

Til hamingju med afmaelisdaginn!
Icelandic

Suk san wan keut!
Thai

Gratulerer med dagen!
Norwegian

Buon compleanno!
Italian

Penblwydd hapus i chi!
Welsh

Yom Huledet Sameach!
Hebrew

Feliz cumpleaños!
Spanish

Roald Dahl says...

'Hunting for wild field-mushrooms is truly one of my favourite pastimes. Mushrooms are very mysterious things. They will grow in one field but not in another and there is no explanation for it. But to walk slowly across a green field in the autumn and spot suddenly ahead of you that little pure white dome nestling in the grass, that, I tell you, is exciting.'

WARNING

POISON

Do NOT eat any mushrooms or toadstools that you find in the wild as many of them can be highly poisonous. Get them checked by an expert first.

Mushrooms that can KILL you!

Fly Agaric – the classic red mushroom with white spots that you see in fairy stories

Devil's Bolete – creamy white and smells unpleasant

Deadly Galerina – dark brown and slimy

Death Cap – yellowish green and smells sickly sweet

Destroying Angel – white, but smells sickly sweet

Q: Why did the mushroom go to the party?
A: *Because he was a fungi*

How to tell a mushroom from a toadstool

– some things to look out for

Mushrooms usually grow in open fields, not under trees or shrubs like toadstools.

The upper part of a mushroom – the cap – should be white and smooth with no scales or warts. Toadstools will often have a different coloured cap with scales and raised lumps on it.

The cap of a true mushroom pulls away from the stem as it grows, which leaves a ring of tissue round the stem. If you can't find a ring of tissue, it's not a true mushroom.

The undersurface of both mushroom and toadstool caps has gills. In a young mushroom these are pink, but they turn brown to almost black as the mushroom matures. Toadstools or poisonous mushrooms have gills that remain white throughout their entire life cycle.

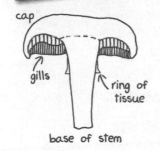

MUSHROOM

cap

gills

ring of tissue

base of stem

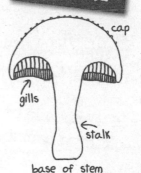

TOADSTOOL

cap

gills

stalk

base of stem

WARNING

Do NOT eat any mushrooms or toadstools that you find in the wild as many of them can be highly poisonous. Get them checked by an expert first.

POISON

Roald Dahl Day
13 September

Even though Roald Dahl is no longer around, his fans plan to celebrate his birthday. One way is to do the Roald Dahl Challenge: ten fun activities inspired by Roald Dahl himself.

1. Wear something yellow – it was his favourite colour.

2. Wear one or more items of clothing backwards.

3. Gobblefunk! (In other words, use the unique language created by Roald Dahl and spoken by the BFG.)

4. Swap a Roald Dahl book with a friend.

5. Talk backwards. Ysae os reve s'ti!

6. Tell a silly joke – Roald Dahl loved swapping these with his children.

7. Play an unexpected prank.

8. Give someone a treat – Roald was a great believer in treats, whether it was a bar of chocolate or a lovely surprise.

9. Write your own revolting rhyme.

10. Make up an Oompa-Loompa dance and get all your friends to join in.

Roald Dahl says...

'It is no good knocking down conkers in August because they are still soft and white. But in September, ah, yes, then they are a deep rich brown colour and shining as though they have been polished and that is the time to gather them by the bucketful.'

What is a Conker?

A conker is a hard, shiny, dark-brown nut that falls from the horse-chestnut tree at this time of year.

Q: What do you call the chocolate factory owner who sits in a horse-chestnut tree?

A: Willy Conker!

Q: What do you call a tree with a croaky voice?

A: A hoarse chestnut.

How to play conkers

This is a game of accuracy and skill, in which players take it in turns to hit each other's conkers.

What you need:

☆ Two players
☆ Two lengths of string
☆ Two conkers

What you do:

1. Each player makes a hole in their conker with a skewer, then threads it on to a piece of string, knotting it securely.

2. The **first player** wraps the end of the string round their hand, allowing the conker to hang down. It must be perfectly still.

3. **The opponent** – known as **the striker** – also wraps the end of the string round their hand, then pulls back the conker with the other hand before attempting to strike the hanging conker.

4. If the striker misses, they are allowed two more shots.

5. If the strings tangle, the first player to shout **'strings!'** gets another go.

6. And if a conker falls to the ground, it's perfectly legal for the striker to shout **'stamps'** and stamp on it as hard as they can – unless the conker's owner gets in first with **'No stamps!'**

7. The conker players take turns at being the striker until one of the conkers is destroyed.

How to Score:

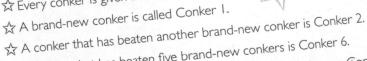

☆ Every conker is given a number.

☆ A brand-new conker is called Conker 1.

☆ A conker that has beaten another brand-new conker is Conker 2.

☆ A conker that has beaten five brand-new conkers is Conker 6.

☆ But, if this Conker 6 beats a Conker 3, then it would become Conker 10. One point is added for the conker victory, plus another three points for the beaten conker's previous score.

The great conker quiz

1 Is a great conker . . .

a one that has been soaked in vinegar for a week?

b one that has been baked in the oven at a low temperature for six hours?

c one that has been stored in a dry place for at least a year?

2 What is the best shape for a conker?

a A flat, sharp-edged one.

b An oval one.

c A big round one.

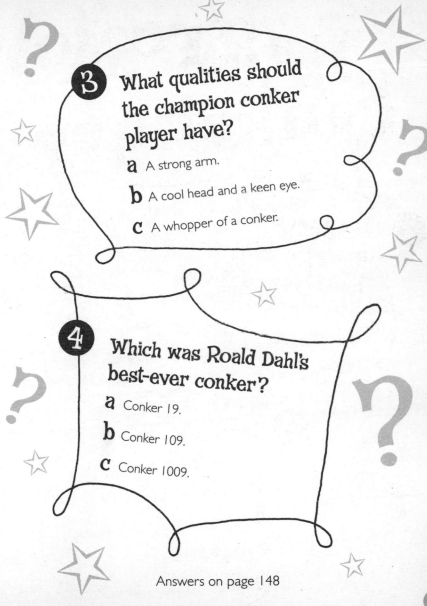

3 What qualities should the champion conker player have?

a A strong arm.

b A cool head and a keen eye.

c A whopper of a conker.

4 Which was Roald Dahl's best-ever conker?

a Conker 19.

b Conker 109.

c Conker 1009.

Answers on page 148

Back to School

Q: Why did the teacher put the lights on?

A: Because the class was so dim.

Q: Did you hear about the cross-eyed teacher?

A: He couldn't control his pupils.

October

See page 26

Roald Dahl's youngest sister →

Another younger sister

St. Peter's
Weston-Super-mare

Dear (Asta,)
            Thanks awfully for your letter and
the comb. When your rabbits were shot, did'nt
Lena hear the shooting, if you get some more
I don't suppose you'll ~~leave~~ put them in
the same place.
Will you remind Mama not to forget ~~my~~ the
(roler) skates, (a man's pair)
I expect as you read this you will either be
sucking your thum in Mama's bed, or you will
be in your own, with (Else) leaning over you, and
saying "Let's see".
            Well, don't forget to tell Mama
about the ROLER skates.
                        love from
                        Roald

Halloween

Halloween takes place on 31 October. It's the scariest night of the year, when spirits and spooks and ghouls walk among us. This makes it the perfect time to read Roald Dahl's *The Witches*. That's if you dare, of course.

Did you know?

Halloween is short for
ALL HALLOW EVEN
(hallow means 'holy') so called because it's the night before All Saints' Day.

MOST HAUNTED PLACES IN THE BRITISH ISLES

THE TOWER OF LONDON, ENGLAND – once a prison and a place where royal prisoners were executed, so it's no wonder ghosts have been seen here. The most famous are Anne Boleyn, the second wife of King Henry VIII, and the Princes in the Tower (two little boys walking hand in hand). Many of the ghosts – including a troop of soldiers and a bear – are seen standing at different tower windows or walking through walls.

BORLEY RECTORY, ESSEX, ENGLAND – once known as the most haunted house in England, there were phantom footsteps, spooky whispers and eerie lights. A ghostly nun was a frequent visitor too.

BALGONIE CASTLE, FIFE, SCOTLAND – Green Jeannie (so called because she is said to be a fetching shade of green) wanders around Scotland's most haunted castle in the small hours of the morning.

THE PROMENADE, PRESTATYN, WALES – keep a lookout for the White Lady of Prestatyn, who is often seen taking a twilight stroll beside the seaside.

KILLAKEE HOUSE, CO DUBLIN, IRELAND – the Black Cat of Killakee once haunted this place, its blazing red eyes terrifying anyone unlucky enough to cross its path ...

Roald Dahl says...

'This, like September, is a lovely month, mild and misty and smelling of ripe apples. We have a small orchard of about five acres at the back of our house and when I first came here nearly forty years ago there were seventy huge old fruit-trees filling the whole field. There were apples, pears, cherries and plums and all of them must have been there since the last century. There was so much fruit every autumn that I told all the children in the village they could come in at any time and ask to borrow a ladder and pick what they wanted. They came in droves.'

Bobbing for apples

This is one of the oldest and most traditional Halloween games.

All you need is:

☆ A large bowl
☆ Water
☆ Apples
☆ A pair of teeth, preferably your own.

Fill a bowl with water and throw in a few apples. Then put your hands behind your back and try to pick up an apple using only your teeth.

WARNING
You might get seriously wet.

Did you know?

The **Romans** brought the apple tree to Britain.

Q: How do you make an apple turnover?

A: Push it down a hill.

Q: What's worse than biting into an apple and finding a worm?

A: Finding half a worm.

True or false?

Liquorice bootlaces are made from rats' blood.

False (probably)

Even though a friend told him that liquorice bootlaces were made by boiling, stirring, crunching, steamrollering and slicing

10,000 rats

into long, thin, red strands, Roald carried on eating them. They were delicious.

liquorice

Bootlaces

Back in time

At 1 a.m. precisely on the last Sunday of October, the clocks go back an hour. British Summer Time is officially over. But there is a bonus – you get a whole extra hour. Here are some suggestions for things to do in it:

☆ Learn to rollerskate.

☆ Dive into a book – not your favourite, most well-thumbed one, but one that you've *never* read before.

☆ Practise saying 'happy birthday' in different languages (see pages 4–5).

☆ Learn to juggle. Start with two balls and move on to three.

'Spring forward, fall back'

A cunning phrase to remind you which way the clocks move in spring and in autumn. In spring, the clocks *spring forward* an hour. In fall (the American way of saying autumn – because the leaves *fall* off the trees), the clocks *fall back* an hour.

Greenwich Mean Time

Wherever you are in the world, all time is measured against the time at Greenwich in London. For example, the time in Hong Kong, China, is said to be 8 hours ahead of Greenwich Mean Time (GMT). New York City, USA, is 5 hours behind GMT. At twelve noon precisely in Greenwich and the rest of the UK, tell the time around the world with this handy timetable:

2 a.m.
Honolulu, Hawaii, USA

4 a.m.
San Francisco, USA

6 a.m.
Mexico City, Mexico

7 a.m.
Québec, Canada

9 a.m.
Buenos Aires, Argentina

12 noon
London, UK

1 p.m.
Berlin, Germany

2 p.m.
Cairo, Egypt

3 p.m.
Moscow, Russia

3.30 p.m.
Tehran, Iran

5.30 p.m.
Mumbai, India

8 p.m.
Beijing, China

10 p.m.
Sydney, Australia

10 ways to spot REAL WITCHES

– according to Roald Dahl

1. They are always women.

2. Instead of fingernails, they have thin curvy claws, like a cat.

3. They wear gloves all the time – except when they are in bed.

4. They are bald.

5. They wear first-class wigs …

6. … and those wigs set up a frightful itch on their bald scalps.

7. They have slightly larger nose-holes than ordinary people …

8. … for smelling children with.

9. They have no toes.

10. They have blue spit.

Did you know?

In the seventeenth century, just after the Civil War, people in the UK were convinced witches really existed. Men were actually employed to ride around the country, sniffing out witches and sending them for trial. The chief of these was called **Matthew Hopkins**. He was known as the

WITCHFINDER GENERAL.

2 OF THE MOST COMMON TESTS FOR WITCHES

Witchmarks: unusual moles, birthmarks or warts were thought to be Devil's Marks and, if poked with a pin, would not bleed or cause pain. Matthew Hopkins had a 'jabbing needle' with a 7.5cm-long spike which retracted into the spring-loaded handle. Not surprisingly, he found a lot of witches!

The water test: an accused witch had her thumbs tied to her opposite big toes (left hand to right foot) and was flung into the river or a handy pond. If she floated she was guilty; if she sank she was innocent. So she lost either way!

Q: What do the Oompa-Loompas celebrate on 31 October?
A: *Marshmalloween!*

Q: How does a Real Witch relax?
A: In a hubble bubble bath.

Q: How do Real Witches diet?
A: *They go to Weight Witches.*

Q: How do Real Witches make their wigs go wild?
A: *With scare-spray.*

November

Time for fireworks and Bonfire Night!

November 9th 1925

No I

Dear Mama

S⁰ Peters
Weston-super-mare

Thank you for your letter. We had a lovely time on thursday, that ½ Mount veuvies was the prettyest I hat first it made a gold fountain and then a silver one, and we had big bonfire with a guy on top, and another of the prettyest of my fireworks was the snow storm, it lit up the hole place.

See page 32

See page 33

The Gunpowder Plot

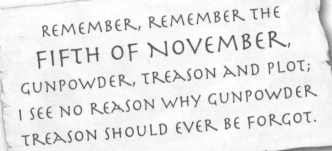

REMEMBER, REMEMBER THE FIFTH OF NOVEMBER, GUNPOWDER, TREASON AND PLOT; I SEE NO REASON WHY GUNPOWDER TREASON SHOULD EVER BE FORGOT.

On **5 November 1605**, Guy Fawkes and twelve other conspirators tried to blow up the Houses of Parliament. Thirty-six barrels of gunpowder were hidden in cellars beneath Parliament, but at the last minute some of the plotters began to have second thoughts. One even sent a letter to an MP friend, warning him to stay at home on 5 November. The letter reached the attention of the king and the gunpowder was discovered – and Guy Fawkes with it. That night, bonfires were lit around the country to celebrate the plot's failure. Guy Fawkes was not burnt on a bonfire like the stuffed guys nowadays, but was instead hanged, drawn and quartered – a very nasty end.

Roald Dahl says...

'Oh, how we used to look forward to the fifth of November at boarding school. In these enlightened times, no one will believe the things we were allowed to do on that famous night . . . boys from seven to twelve years old all setting off their own fireworks with their own matches. Pretty lethal fireworks too.'

WE FORK SIR*

Can you unscramble the names of Roald Dahl's favourite fireworks?

 A CALM DR NEON

 CO TREK

 BRACKEN CRAG

 A NERD LOG IN

 REPENT FIRES

Answers on page 148

* FIREWORKS, of course!

10 things you might not know about volcanoes

For real explosions, check out these volcanic facts:

1. When a volcano erupts, it can shoot ash as far as 40km into the air.

2. The biggest volcano in the world is Mauna Loa in Hawaii. It is over 8km high, though some of it is underwater.

3. The most active volcano in the world is Kilauea in Hawaii. It has been erupting almost non-stop since 1983.

4. Roald Dahl's screenplay for the 1967 James Bond film, *You Only Live Twice*, included a top-secret hideaway inside a volcano, complete with an evil baddy and a monorail.

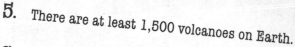

5. There are at least 1,500 volcanoes on Earth.

6. About 150 volcanoes erupt every year.

7. When Vesuvius – Italy's most famous volcano – erupted in AD 79, it buried the nearby towns of Herculaneum and Pompeii under tonnes of ash.

8. The area around the Pacific Ocean where earthquakes and volcanic eruptions are common is called the Ring of Fire.

9. A volcanic eruption usually lasts between ten and 100 days.

10. When Mount St Helens, Washington, erupted in 1980, it was one of the USA's biggest volcanic explosions ever.

Roald Dahl says...

'For many small animals, the approach of winter means the time to go to sleep until spring arrives again. It would make life a lot more comfortable if we could do the same.'

True or false?

Grass snakes hug each other to keep warm in winter.

True

They have no real homes and simply hide themselves among the twisted tree roots underneath hedges. Quite often they will coil themselves round each other for comfort.

Recipe for Savoury Crocodile

This is a **recipe** from **Quentin Blake**.

The **first** Roald Dahl book he **illustrated** was

The Enormous Crocodile, published in 1978.

SAUSAGES

GHERKIN

What you will need:

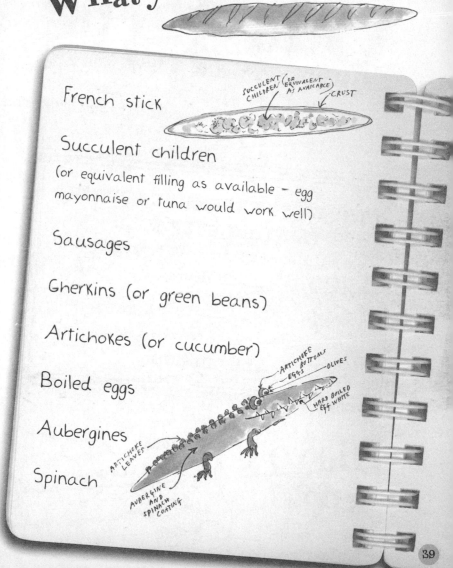

French stick

SUCCULENT (OR EQUIVALENT AS AVAILABLE)
CHILDREN
CRUST

Succulent children

(or equivalent filling as available – egg mayonnaise or tuna would work well)

Sausages

Gherkins (or green beans)

Artichokes (or cucumber)

ARTICHOKE
BOTTOMS
OLIVES
EGGS
HARD BOILED
EGG WHITE

Boiled eggs

Aubergines

ARTICHOKE
LEAVES

Spinach

AUBERGINE
AND
SPINACH
COATING

Odd^{arty}h facts

Roald Dahl loved to collect fine art
and beautiful paintings.
Here are some odd facts that might have intrigued him.

THE MOST EXPENSIVE BRITISH PAINTING EVER SOLD

In April 2006, a painting of Venice by J. M. W. Turner was sold for

£20.5 million at Christie's, New York.

The most expensive painting ever is Picasso's *Garçon
à la Pipe (Boy with a Pipe)*, sold in New York in 2004 for

£59 million.

Did you know?

In **1888** the famous painter **Vincent Van Gogh** (he painted *Sunflowers*) cut off part of his left ear and gave it to someone as a present.

THE MOST FAMOUS PAINTING IN THE WORLD

The **Mona Lisa** by **Leonardo da Vinci** is generally considered to be the most famous painting in the history of art. It was painted between **1503** and **1505** and is a portrait of a real woman, Monna (or Mona) Lisa, who was married to Francesco del Giacondo -- which explains the other name of the painting: *La Giaconda*. In 2004, the painting was valued at over $608 million! However, many people consider it to be priceless.

The man who stole the *Mona Lisa*

On **21 August 1911**, the *Mona Lisa* was stolen from the **Louvre museum** in Paris. The police searched the museum from top to bottom (which took a week because it is so large) but the only thing they found was the heavy frame. Two years later, the thief was identified when an Italian called **Vincenzo Perugia** tried to sell the painting to the **Uffizi Gallery** in Florence for **$100,000**. Apparently he had hidden overnight in the Louvre, then, when the museum was closed, had unhooked the painting from the wall and cut it out of its frame. While trying to leave the building, he came to a locked door. He simply unscrewed the doorknob, put it in his pocket and walked outside with the world's most famous painting under his jacket.

A Sad day

Roald Dahl died on **23 November 1990** at the age of seventy-four. The last two books he wrote were published after his death. They were *The Vicar of Nibbleswicke* and *The Minpins*.

Did you know?

Roald Dahl thought the best book he ever wrote was *The BFG*. Do you agree?

December

Dec. 12th. 1926.

St. Peter's
Weston-super-mare.

Dear Mama,

This is my last letter to you this term. We had a special treat east night, we all hung up our stockings, and when it was dark matron came in dressed up as (father xmas) and put things in our stockings, I got a kind of a musical box and a soldier on a horse in mine. the same night she hung up hers out side her door and we all put things in it, it was full in the end. We start Escams next Tuesday and they go on till Thursday. I AM COMING HOME NEXT FRIDAY

See page 50

Happy birthday, Quentin!

Quentin Blake was born on 16 December 1932 in Sidcup, Kent. His first drawing was published when he was just sixteen and he went on to illustrate a huge number of children's books – including all but one of Roald Dahl's (The Minpins is the exception). He has also written and illustrated many of his own titles.

10 things you might not know about Quentin Blake

1. He started drawing when he was five years old.

2. He liked school and once learnt to be a teacher. (He's actually a proper professor.)

3. When he is drawing someone's expression he pulls the same face himself.

4. He was nervous about first meeting Roald Dahl, but they soon became the best of friends.

5. Quentin draws lots of roughs before completing his final drawing.

6. His favourite Roald Dahl book is *The BFG*.

7. Of his own books, he likes *Clown* best.

8. Roald Dahl once sent Quentin a sandal through the post to show him what the BFG's footwear should look like.

9. In 1999 Quentin became the very first Children's Laureate and spent the next two years doing everything he could to promote children's literature.

10. Roald Dahl called him Quent.

To find out even more about the fantastic Quentin Blake, visit his website:
quentinblake.com

What Roald Dahl thought about Quentin Blake

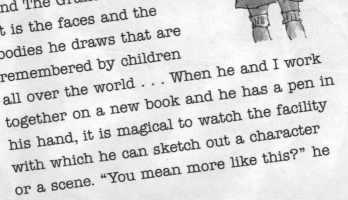

'. . . It is Quent's pictures rather than my own written descriptions that have brought to life such characters as the BFG, Miss Trunchbull, Mr Twit and The Grand High Witch. It is the faces and the bodies he draws that are remembered by children all over the world . . . When he and I work together on a new book and he has a pen in his hand, it is magical to watch the facility with which he can sketch out a character or a scene. "You mean more like this?" he will say, and the nib will fly over the paper at incredible speed, making thin lines in black ink, and in thirty seconds he has produced a new picture. "Perhaps," I will say, "he should have a more threatening look about him." Once again the pen flies over the paper and there before you is exactly what you are after. But this is not to say that I "help" him with many of the characters he draws for my books. Most of them he does entirely on his own and they are far better and funnier than anything I could think of.'

ROald Dahl says...

'In December, the tawny owls in our orchard start hooting like mad all through the night. You will quite often also hear them if you live in a town where they exist by pouncing on starlings and sparrows while they are roosting and fast asleep.'

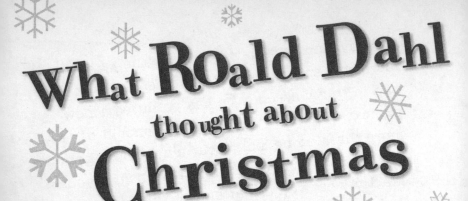

What Roald Dahl thought about Christmas

Roald Dahl loved giving presents, but he hated Christmas. Here's what he thought about it:

1. Christmas is for children.

2. Grown-ups should try to make Christmas fun for children.

3. Christmas is a bonanza for shopkeepers. Everyone else gets poor.

4. Home-made Christmas cards are the best things ever.

5. Christmas cards with photos of the senders on the front are the worst things ever.

6. Presents should be given to family members and no one else.

7. Goose tastes wonderful . . .

8. . . . but turkey is one of the most tasteless meats that it is possible to find.

9. The best presents of all are the simplest ones.

10. One of Roald Dahl's favourite presents was a glass jar of wine gums given to him by his daughter Ophelia.

Did you know?

In **Sweden** and **Finland**, it was once ruled that anyone breaking the law on any of the twelve days of Christmas (25 December to 5 January) would receive a harsher sentence than at any other time of the year.

Q: What do snowmen eat for breakfast?
A: Snowflakes.

Q: What does Father Christmas do in his garden?
A: Hoe hoe hoe!

Q: Why are Christmas trees like bad knitters?
A: They both drop their needles on the carpet.

Q: What happens to Father Christmas if he gets stuck up the chimney?
A: *He gets Santa Claustrophobia.*

Q: What happens if you eat Christmas decorations?
A: *You get tinselitis.*

Top 10 Christmas firsts

1. The first **Christmas card** was sent in the UK in **1843**.

2. The first **charity Christmas card** was sent in **1949** – all profits went to UNICEF (the United Nations Children's Fund).

3. The picture of **Father Christmas** as we know him today – a jolly round man in a red and white suit – first appeared in a **1931** Coca-Cola advert drawn by Haddon Sundblom. Before then, the Victorians had shown him wearing red, blue, green or brown. In the US, he had worn red, but he had been an elf, not a human. If you've seen him, you'll know of course what he looks like!

4. The first **Christmas cracker** was pulled in **1846**.

5. The first **advent calendar** was made in Germany in **1851** . . .

6. . . . but the first **chocolate-filled advent calendar** wasn't produced until a whole century later!

7. In **1834**, Prince Albert – Queen Victoria's husband – introduced the first **Christmas tree** to Windsor Castle. Soon, the rest of the UK joined in.

8. The first **Christmas fairy lights** appeared just three years after Thomas Edison invented the light bulb. One of the American inventor's friends – Edward Johnson – used them to decorate his tree in **1882**.

9. **Tinsel** was invented in Germany in **1610**. The first garland was made of real silver.

10. The first **English collection of carols** was published in **1521**, but they were probably sung much earlier than that.

What was in Roald Dahl's cellar?

Cases and cases of wine!

Roald Dahl loved wine, and his large cellar, with a constant temperature of 12.8°C, summer and winter, was an ideal storing place. Some years are better than others as far as wine-making is concerned. **1982** was a very good year for wine and Roald bought 1,000 cases (with 12 bottles in a case, that's a great party!). Then, because the way down to his cellar was long and steep, he had to have a wooden chute made so that he could slide the cases into place rather than carry them.

Other really good years for wine were:

1959, 1961, 1990, 2000.

Did you know?

Conventional wine is made from grapes, but you can make wine from practically anything, including parsnips, beetroot, dandelions, carrots and potatoes. Anyone for a glass of swede?

January

Asta, Roald's youngest sister

See page 60

Sᵗ Peter's,
Weston-super-mare.
January 27ᵗʰ, 1926.

Dear Baby

We had a fine game of ruggar yesterday, I was one of the captain's, they beat us ~~24~~ 21 points to 1, but we had all the ~~little ones~~ smaller boys on our side except one or two, we got awful ey dirty we got splashed all over with mud, to day we go for a run, you see we ~~go~~ run about ~~three~~ 1½ miles and then run back, we do that once a week to get pratcis but we'r awfuly stiff the next morning.

Roald Dahl says...

'As the clock approaches midnight on the thirty-first of December you are still in the old year, but then all at once, one millionth of a second after midnight, you are in the new ... The same sort of thing happens on your birthday when you are nine years old one day and ten years old the next. It is lovely to be a year older, but it is the suddenness of it all that is so amazing.'

New Year's resolutions:

Can you match these Roald Dahl characters with the New Year's resolutions they might have made?

1. 'To repair the chocolate-factory roof.'

2. 'To read *Encyclopaedia Britannica*. All of it.'

3. 'To win first prize in a giant fruit and vegetable competition.'

4. 'Not to eat cabbage soup – not this year, not next year, not ever again!'

5. 'To inspect spaghetti suppers very thoroughly before a single strand passes my lips.'

Answers on page 148

How did the months get their names?

January – named after Janus, the two-faced Roman god who looked backwards and forwards

February – named after the Roman feast, *februa*, always held in this month

March – once the first month of the Roman year, it was named after Mars, the god of war

April – from the Latin word *aperire*, meaning 'to open'. It is traditionally a month of new growth, when buds open and plants come to life after winter

May – named after Maia, the goddess of growth

June – named after Juno, the goddess of young women

July – named in honour of Julius Caesar, a famous Roman general who conquered Britain. He was later stabbed to death

August – named after another Roman general, this time Caesar Augustus

September – from the Latin *septum*, which means 'seven'. Even though September is the ninth month of the year, it used to be the seventh month of the Roman calendar

October – from the Latin *octo*, which means 'eight', because it used to be the eighth month of the Roman year

November – from the Latin *novem*, which means 'nine'

December – from the Latin *decem*, which means 'ten'

Roald Dahl
and the dragon!

According to the Chinese calendar, each year is named after a different animal – twelve animals in all. Roald Dahl was born in the Year of the Dragon. Which year were you born in?

Year of the Rat
1948, 1960, 1972, 1984, 1996

Year of the Ox
1949, 1961, 1973, 1985, 1997

Year of the Tiger
1950, 1962, 1974, 1986, 1998

Year of the Hare
1951, 1963, 1975, 1987, 1999

Year of the Dragon
1952, 1964, 1976, 1988, 2000

Year of the Snake
1953, 1965, 1977, 1989, 2001

Year of the Horse
1954, 1966, 1978, 1990, 2002

Year of the Sheep
1955, 1967, 1979, 1991, 2003

Year of the Monkey
1956, 1968, 1980, 1992, 2004

Year of the Rooster
1957, 1969, 1981, 1993, 2005

Year of the Dog
1958, 1970, 1982, 1994, 2006

Year of the Pig
1959, 1971, 1983, 1995, 2007

3 Sports that Roald Dahl enjoyed

At school young Roald played sports all year round, even in freezing cold January. It was fortunate that he was good at sport and even more fortunate that he liked it. Here are some of his favourites.

Squash-rackets

This is the old-fashioned name for squash. It's a bit like playing tennis inside a house. With smaller rackets. And a smaller ball.

Eton-fives

This is a handball game that's played in a three-sided court by two teams of two players. The object of the game is to whack a small, hard ball around the court. To be a top player, you have to be lightning quick. Luckily, Roald Dahl was.

Rugby

Roald Dahl called this rugger. A rugby ball is that odd shape because it used to be made from a pig's bladder. When the bladder was puffed full of air – not a popular job – it formed an oval shape rather than a perfect sphere. Nowadays rugby balls are made from rubber. Pigs everywhere heave a sigh of relief!

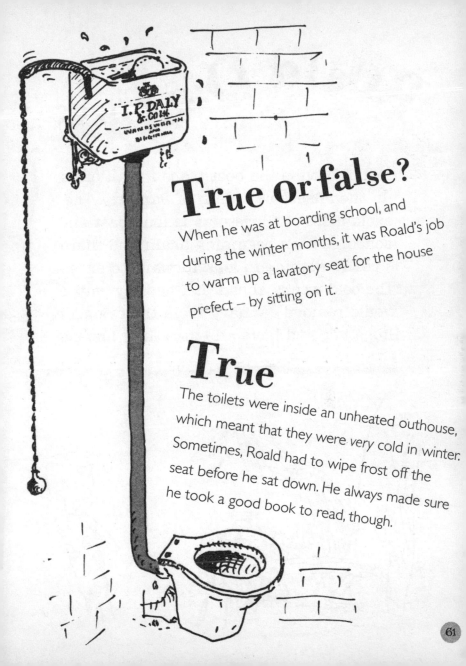

True or false?

When he was at boarding school, and during the winter months, it was Roald's job to warm up a lavatory seat for the house prefect – by sitting on it.

True

The toilets were inside an unheated outhouse, which meant that they were very cold in winter. Sometimes, Roald had to wipe frost off the seat before he sat down. He always made sure he took a good book to read, though.

Roald Dahl says...

'A hot bath is the best place for all of us in the miserable month of January. The excitement of Christmas is long past and school is soon beginning again and there is really nothing to look forward to except the cold weeks ahead. If I had my way, I would remove January from the calendar altogether and have an extra July instead.'

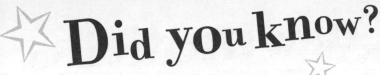

Did you know?

In January each year, the most popular library books and their authors are announced. Here's a list of the top ten most-borrowed children's authors for 2004–5:

1. Jacqueline Wilson
2. Mick Inkpen
3. Janet & Allan Ahlberg
4. **Roald Dahl**
5. Lucy Daniels
6. Enid Blyton
7. Nick Butterworth
8. Eric Hill
9. Lucy Cousins
10. Rose Impey

Of all Roald Dahl's books, *George's Marvellous Medicine* was borrowed most often – over 30,000 times. (That means someone took out a copy every 17.47 minutes!)

A new medicine

'So-ho! thought George suddenly. *Ah-ha!*
Ho-hum! I know exactly what I'll do. I
shall make her a *new* medicine, one that
is so strong and so fierce and so fantastic
it will either cure her completely or blow
off the top of her head. I'll make her a
magic medicine, a medicine no doctor
in the world has ever made before.'

Real marvellous medicines

In 1798, English doctor Edward Jenner discovered that if he injected the fluid from cowpox blisters into the skin of healthy people, they were immunized against the deadly smallpox virus. **He had discovered the very first** vaccine.

American dentist William Morton was credited with the first successful use of **anaesthetic** during an operation in 1846. However, Crawford Long – an American surgeon – had been using anaesthetic since 1842.

English surgeon and scientist Joseph Lister discovered that it was vitally important to keep operation wounds absolutely clean to avoid infection. He first used antiseptic **to clean wounds and surgeons' hands in 1865.**

In 1902, Polish-born French physicist Marie Curie isolated the chemical element **radium**, which was used to treat cancer.

In 1928, Scottish bacteriologist Alexander Fleming discovered the antibiotic **called penicillin in a mouldy old dish in his lab. It is now used to treat infection and disease. Fleming won the Nobel Prize for his marvellous medical breakthrough.**

Q: Where did James, Old-Green-Grasshopper, Spider, Ladybird, Silkworm, Centipede, Earthworm and Glow-Worm play soccer?

A: On a giant football peach.

Q: What do you say to Mr Twit when he has stale bread, baked beans and smelly sardines poking out of his ears?

A: Anything you like – he can't hear you.

Q: What do you call a very clever girl who's an expert ballroom dancer?

A: Waltzing Matilda.

February

St Peter's
Weston-super-mare.
Feb 17th 1925

Dear Baby

We had pancakes yesterday because it was (pancake day) and the cook took from 10 o'clock to half dinner time to make pancakes for all of us, because every one had to be made separately, but they were very nice, the cook said to Mr Frances he was glad pancake day was not every day. Give my love to everyone. Love from

BoY

See page 72

Roald Dahl says...

'Is February, we ask ourselves, any better than January? Well, yes, in a way it is because you know that if only you can get through it and put it behind you, then the worst of the winter is probably over. On the other hand, this is usually the fiercest and bitterest month of all. I treat February like a school term and keep counting how many days there are left until it is over.'

February weather around the world

	Average high (°C)	Average low (°C)	Average rain/snow (mm)
Alexandria, Egypt	19	11	23
Athens, Greece	14	7	37
Dar Es Salaam, Tanzania	31	25	66
Edinburgh, Scotland	6	1	39
Hong Kong, China	17	13	46
London, England	7	2	40
Melbourne, Australia	26	14	46
New York City, USA	3	-4	97
Oslo, Norway	-7	-7	35
Vancouver, Canada	7	1	147

Weather data compiled from:
http://www.bbc.co.uk/weather/world/city_guides/

Roald Dahl's favourite things

Come rain, shine, frost or snow, Roald Dahl could be found inside the shed at the end of his garden. This was where he wrote. And beside him there was a table where he kept his most favourite things. They're all still there.

Here are some of the items on Roald Dahl's table:

1. A ball made from silver chocolate wrappers.
2. A small model of a Hurricane fighter plane.
3. His hipbone.
4. A glass bottle filled with mauve-coloured bits of gristle taken from Roald Dahl's spine during an operation.
5. A photo of his granddaughter, Sophie.
6. A meteorite the size of a golf ball.
7. His father's silver and tortoiseshell paper-knife.
8. A solar-powered musical box.
9. A carving of a green grasshopper.
10. A cone from a cedar tree.

Roald Dahl films

Do you know which of Roald Dahl's books have been made into films? Here's a list:

Willy Wonka and the Chocolate Factory

(1971) – starring Gene Wilder

The BFG

(1989) – with voices by David Jason, Amanda Root and Angela Thorne

Danny the Champion of the World

(1989, made for TV) – starring Jeremy Irons, Robbie Coltrane, Michael Hordern and Lionel Jeffries

The Witches

(1990) – starring Angelica Huston, Mai Zetterling and Rowan Atkinson

James and the Giant Peach

(1996) – with voices by Simon Callow, Richard Dreyfuss, Joanna Lumley and Susan Sarandon

Matilda

(1996) – starring Mara Wilson, Danny DeVito and Pam Ferris

Charlie and the Chocolate Factory

(2005) – starring Johnny Depp, Freddy Highmore and Helena Bonham Carter

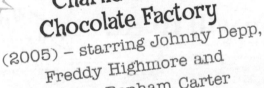

Did you know?

Roald Dahl co-wrote the screenplays for the James Bond film *You Only Live Twice* (1967) and *Chitty Chitty Bang Bang* (1968) too.

How to make
pancakes

Pancake Day, also known as Shrove Tuesday, usually takes place this month. Here's how to make them — **but ask an adult to help as cooking can be dangerous.**

What you will need:

They're flipping good!

☆ 140g plain flour
☆ 284ml milk*
☆ 1 egg
☆ A bowl
☆ A whisk or a blender
☆ A non-stick frying pan
☆ A spatula
☆ A handy adult

* If you want to make orange-flavoured pancakes, squeeze the juice out of two oranges and add enough milk to make 284ml of liquid. Then make the pancakes exactly the same way. To make them *really* tasty, add a splash of orange juice and a drizzle of chocolate sauce when they're done. Mmm ...

What you do:

1. Put all the ingredients in a bowl and whisk them together to make a sloppy batter. (If you have a blender, whizz the ingredients in one of these instead.)

2. Heat the frying pan on the hob, adding a knob of butter when it's hot.

3. When the frying pan is smoking hot, pour in half a cup of batter and quickly swirl it around.

4. Wait a few seconds, then loosen the edges with a spatula and shake the frying pan to make sure that the pancake doesn't stick.

5. After about a minute, FLIP the pancake up and over. Or turn it over with a spatula (you're more likely to end up with the pancake in the frying pan, but less likely to impress an audience).

6. When the pancake has cooked on the other side, eat with freshly squeezed lemon and a sprinkling of sugar.

Roald Dahl says...

'I have always regarded the mole as a friend because he eats all the horrid centipedes and leatherjackets and other pests that damage our flowers and vegetables . . . But I will tell you a very simple method of persuading a mole to leave your garden or your field. Moles cannot stand noise of any sort. It makes them even more nervous than they already are. So when I see a molehill in the garden, I get an empty wine bottle (plenty of those around in our house) and I bury it in the ground close to the molehill, leaving only the neck of the bottle sticking up. Now when the wind blows across the open top of the bottle it makes a soft humming sound. This goes on all day and night because there is almost always some sort of a breeze blowing. The constant noise just above his tunnel drives the mole half crazy and he very soon packs up and goes somewhere else. This is not a joke. It really works. I have done it often.'

True or false?

Only female mosquitoes bite people.

True

Goodness knows why. They just do.

Did you know?

A mole can dig approximately a metre of tunnel in an hour.

Valentine's Day

14 February is St Valentine's Day – officially the most romantic day of the year since the fourteenth century. However, it was not until the mid-nineteeth century that Valentine cards began to be popular, a craze begun by Esther Howland in the USA. Now approximately one billion Valentine's cards are sent every year.

Big Friendly Giants

The BFG had something in common with Roald Dahl. He was incredibly tall. Roald Dahl himself measured 1.98 metres (6 feet 6 inches). Here are more big friendly giants:

Robert Wadlow
(tallest man ever)
2.72 metres

Xi Shun
(tallest living man)
2.36 metres

Peter Mayhew
(Chewbacca of *Star Wars*)
2.21 metres

Michael Crichton
(author of *Jurassic Park*)
2.06 metres

Dave Prowse
(Darth Vader of *Star Wars*)
2.01 metres

Peter the Great
(Russian king)
2.01 metres

Christopher Lee
(Saruman in
Lord of the Rings)
1.96 metres

John Cleese
(actor and comedian)
1.95 metres

March

St Peter's

Weston-super-mare.

March. 24th 1926.

Dear Else

I will soon be coming home,
I am coming by train next Wedensday.

See
page
80

There is a (craze) for darts and
gliders, nearly every one has got
one, I have got one (topping) one,
it glides like anythig, a boy
called Huntly-Wood made it for
me.

See
page
78

Top word

When Roald Dahl was a boy, *topping* did not mean something that you put on top of a cake or ice cream. It meant 'cool'.

How frightfully topping!

Unexpected happenings

Roald Dahl's *Tales of the Unexpected* were first shown on television in March 1979. These were eerie, ghoulish and very inventive stories with unexpected twists. The programmes were very successful in the UK and the USA.

Good weather for flying kites

March is traditionally a very windy month – perfect for flying kites! Here are some kite facts:

1. Kites first became popular in China, 3,000 years ago.

2. American inventor Benjamin Franklin proved that lightning was a natural phenomenon by flying a kite during a storm.

3. Wilbur and Orville Wright – the first people ever to fly – first tested their biplane designs as kites.

4. Kites have been used to ward off evil, deliver messages, spy, send radio signals and drop leaflets. They've even been flown for fun!

5. Kite-surfing is an exhilarating sport that uses a kite and a surfboard to send the kite-surfer whizzing from wave to wave across the sea.

Crazy crazes

When Roald Dahl was at school, he joined in all the very latest crazes. In the 1920s, these included darts, gliders, stamp-collecting and roller-skating. Since then, there have been many other weird and wonderful crazes, like these:

Hula hoop

(1950s) – a big, plastic hoop that people twirled round and round on their hips

The Twist

(1960s) – a super-twisty dance, where your top half swivels the other way from your bottom half

Lava lamps

(1960s) – not real lava, but lamps filled with blippity-blopping gloop

Pet rocks

(1970s) – dreamt up by a fellow called Gary Dahl (no relation to Roald), these were small grey pebbles that people treated as pets. The craze didn't last long, but it made the other Dahl a fortune

Space Hopper

(1970s) – a large orange blow-up ball with ears to hang on to while you bounce

Rubik's cube

(1980s) – a mechanical cube-shaped puzzle with moveable, colourful sections

What's the meaning of 'Roald'?

Roald is an Old Norse word that means 'famous'.

Other famous Roalds

Roald Amundsen was a famous Norwegian explorer who took part in one of the most exciting and dangerous races of all time. In 1911, he and Captain Scott – a British explorer – competed against one another to cross the treacherous Antarctic ice in an effort to become the first person to reach the South Pole. Amundsen won, possibly because of the extra spurts of energy provided by his delicious chocolate rations. Harald and Sophie Magdalene Dahl were so impressed by his record-breaking exploits that they named their son after him.

Roald is a small village in Giske, Norway. It is very famous indeed to the 700 people who live there, but Roald Dahl was never one of them.

All Over the World

Roald Dahl's books have been translated into **over 40 different languages** and are sold around the world. Can you recognize the following titles?

1. *Charlie und die Schokoladenfabrik* (German)

2. *Le Bon Gros Géant* (French)

3. *Danny El Campeon Del Mundo* (Spanish)

4. *Le Doigt Magique* (French)

5. *Los Cretinos* (Spanish)

6. *Das Wundermittel* (German)

7. *Agu Trot* (Spanish)

8. *Sophiechen und der Riese* (German)

9. *Charlie Y El Gran Ascensor De Cristal* (Spanish)

10. *Les Deux Gredins* (French)

11. *La Jirafa, El Pelicano Y El Mono* (Spanish)

Answers on page 148

Did you know?

Roald Dahl's favourite composer was Beethoven. Here are a few more musical facts:

☆ **When Beethoven went deaf, he cut off the legs of his piano, so he could feel the vibrations in the floor when he played.**

☆ **The 17th-century French composer Jean-Baptiste Lully died when he stuck the spiked wooden staff he used to beat time into his foot instead of into the floor. The injury was mistreated, gangrene set in and he died from the infection.**

☆ The 18th-century Italian composer Rossini loved eating more than he liked composing. He once wrote that he had only cried three times in his life: when his first opera was a flop, when he heard Paganini play the violin and the day a turkey stuffed with truffles fell overboard on a floating picnic.

☆ The 19th-century French composer Hector Berlioz was in love with two women. They both jilted him, so he decided to murder them. He disguised himself as a lady's maid, and set off from Rome to Paris with two double-barrelled pistols and various poisons. When he arrived in Nice, he got bored with his plan and had a delicious lunch instead.

☆ The 20th-century composer Anton Webern was accidentally shot by an American soldier in 1945 when he stepped outside to light an after-dinner cigar.

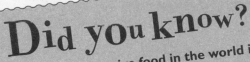

Did you know?

The most expensive food in the world is harvested from the purple crocus, which begins to bloom in March. Saffron is made from the dried orange-red stigmas from inside the flowers and is used to turn rice and cakes bright yellow – as well as giving them a deliciously subtle flavour. But it comes at a price. A gram of saffron costs much more than a gram of chocolate, a gram of smoked salmon and even a gram of caviar.

AN INGENIOUS
(BUT TOTALLY ILLEGAL AND UTTERLY FORBIDDEN)
USE FOR SPRING LAMB

Spring lambs are born in March. And in his short story *Lamb to the Slaughter*, Roald Dahl converts lamb into the most inventive murder weapon ever. A wife hits her husband over the head with a frozen leg of lamb, and then roasts the meat. The detectives who investigate the murder enjoy a slap-up meal – and eat the evidence!

April

APRIL FOOL

Gotcha!

This is an actual April Fool of a letter that Roald Dahl sent to his mother one year. He adored practical jokes.

April Fool

Why do we play April Fool jokes?

The custom may have begun in France when, in 1582, the calendar was adjusted to be more accurate. It meant that New Year's Day was moved from 25 March to 1 January. Anyone who continued to celebrate the end of the New Year week on 1 April was said to be a fool. An April Fool.

Fools beware!

Play as many
April Fool jokes as you like
before noon
on 1 April, but remember that
the person who plays tricks *after*
noon becomes a fool themselves.

5 of the best April Fool jokes ever

1. When a television programme shown in 1957 fooled viewers into thinking that spaghetti grew on trees.

2. When an electronics expert convinced people in 1962 that they could turn their black and white televisions into colour televisions by stretching a pair of tights over the screen.

3. When a man set fire to a pile of tyres inside a dormant volcano in 1974. Black smoke belched into the air, fooling locals that Mount Edgecumbe was about to erupt. (Now that's bad!)

4. When astronomer Patrick Moore told radio listeners that the alignment of planets would create a temporary change in gravity and that if they jumped into the air at precisely 9.47 a.m. on 1 April 1976, they would experience weightlessness.

5. When a burger chain announced in 1998 that they were selling a left-handed burger, designed especially for left-handed people. Thousands flocked to buy them.

Birdspotters, Watch Out!

This is the month that flocks of birds return home after the winter. Look out for:

Skylarks

Greenfinches

Whitethroats

Willow warblers

Goldfinches

Golden plovers

Blackcaps

Swallows

House martins

Chiffchaffs

When is Easter Sunday?

Easter Sunday is usually in April, sometimes in March.
It changes every single year. You can work out yourself
when Easter Sunday will be using a calculator and
a telescope (to check for full moons) . . . or you can
simply consult this chart. Then you'll know when to
look forward to all that lovely chocolate.

8 April 2007

23 March 2008

12 April 2009

4 April 2010

24 April 2011

8 April 2012

31 March 2013

20 April 2014

5 April 2015

27 March 2016

Roald Dahl says...

'There is something incredibly exciting in finding a chocolate egg wrapped in silver paper cunningly hidden in the tuft of the heather plant or in the branches of ivy or in the bole of a hollow tree.'

5 golden rules for organizing an Easter-egg hunt

START

1 Pick your hunting ground carefully – somewhere only you and your friends are going to be.

2 Get yourself a big bag of little chocolate eggs. (And remember ... there's no such thing as *too many* eggs.)

3 Make doubly sure there is no one around when you hide the eggs (very important, this, otherwise your hunt will be very brief).

4 Pick a variety of hiding places for the eggs – some high, some low, some cleverly hidden, some blindingly obvious. (This is a sure-fire way of making sure *everyone* finds some eggs.)

5 All eggs must be hidden by nightfall on Easter Saturday, ready for early risers the next day!

Or better still – get someone else to organize an Easter-egg hunt and then search for the chocolate eggs yourself.

Did you know?

THE AZTEC EMPEROR MONTEZUMA

loved to drink thick chocolate dyed red.
It was served in golden goblets that were
thrown away after only being used once.
The emperor sometimes emptied 50
goblets in a single day ...

Q: How do you turn light chocolate into dark chocolate?

A: Turn the light off.

Q: What's made of chocolate and is found on the sea bed?

A: An oyster egg.

Q: What happened to the egg that was tickled too much?

A: It cracked up.

Q: What's blue, silver, pink, blue, silver and pink?

A: An Easter egg rolling down a hill.

Q: What did the headmaster egg say to the pupil egg?

A: 'I'm going to have to eggspell you.'

What is Chocolate?

It's lovely, that's what it is. Oh, you mean what *is* it? Well . . . Chocolate is a wonderful substance made from roasted and ground cacao seeds, usually sweetened and eaten as confectionery. **It's truly gloriumptious.**

A brief history of chocolate

☆ **6th century AD**
Chocolate was made by the Mayans in Central America from the seed of the cacahuaquchtl tree. The word 'chocolate' comes from their word 'xocoatl', which means 'bitter water'.

☆ **13th century**
The Aztecs used cocoa to make thick, cold chocolate drinks. Sugar was unknown, so they used different spices to flavour the drinks, including hot chilli peppers!

☆ **16th century**
Chocolate was brought to Spain by Hernando Cortez. The Spaniards mixed the beans with sugar, vanilla, nutmeg, cloves and other spices. Suddenly, it was a whole lot tastier. Spain managed to keep chocolate a secret from the rest of the world for almost 100 years.

☆ 17th century

Chocolate became popular in France, especially in the extravagant royal court of Louis XIV. It also reached Italy.

☆ 1657

London's very first chocolate shop opened, followed by many more. They became popular places for fashionable people to meet and chat and drink chocolate.

☆ 1711

Chocolate reached Austria . . .

☆ 1720

. . . and spread to Germany and Switzerland.

☆ 1755

America discovered chocolate. The first US factory opened ten years later.

☆ 1830

The very first chocolate confectionery was created by J. S. Fry & Sons, in Britain.

☆ 1849

The Cadbury brothers exhibited their chocolate in Birmingham.

☆ 1875

Daniel Peter, from Switzerland, produced the first milk chocolate bar.

☆ 1876

The rest is chocolate history.

The Queen's birthday

Her Majesty Queen Elizabeth II was born on 21 April 1926. But she doesn't just celebrate her birthday in April. Oh no. She has more than one. How? See page 112.

May

May 9th 1926.

St Peter's
Weston-super-mare.

Dear Mama

Thank you for the Music Book and the envalopes. I have played (cricket) twice this term, and in the middle it began to rain but not very hard so we were able to go on. On Monday and Tuesday we were alowed to go down to the town or sail our boats in the paddling pool on the sands, or go on the peer, so we had quite a nice time. The (swiming baths) arn't filled yed, but they were soon it be filled so we can bathe.

Love from

B O Y

See page 124

See page 108

☆ May Day ☆

1 May is traditionally the day on which the return of spring is celebrated and farmers wish for good crops in the coming months.

MAYDAY!

Not another bank holiday, but the international radio distress signal used by ships and aircraft to tell anyone nearby that they are in grave danger. So why is it named after a springtime festival? Aha – it isn't! 'Mayday' comes from the French *m'aider*, which means 'help me'!

Q: What's French for 'I am an Australian'?

A: *Moi Aussi.*

Did you know?

The old-fashioned saying 'Ne'er cast a clout till May is out' means that you shouldn't hurry to 'cast a clout' – go without your winter woollies – until the end of this month. Otherwise, May is likely to catch you out with a sudden spell of cold weather.

Roald Dahl Says...

Back at school after the Easter holidays, young Roald used to rely on his trusty tuck-box to remind him of home. 'A tuck-box is a small pinewood trunk which is very strongly made, and no boy has ever gone as a boarder to an English prep school without one. It is his own secret storehouse, as secret as a lady's handbag, and there is an unwritten law that no other boy, no teacher, not even the headmaster himself has the right to pry into the contents of your tuck-box.'

In Roald Dahl's tuck-box

- ☆ Half a home-made currant cake
- ☆ A packet of squashed-fly biscuits
- ☆ A couple of oranges
- ☆ A pot of strawberry jam or Marmite
- ☆ A bar of chocolate
- ☆ A bag of Liquorice Allsorts
- ☆ A magnet
- ☆ A pocketknife
- ☆ A compass
- ☆ A box of conjuring tricks
- ☆ A catapult
- ☆ A couple of stink bombs

Whose lunchbox?

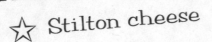

Can you guess which of Roald Dahl's characters might have owned these rather strange lunchboxes?

☆ Stilton cheese

☆ Tinned sardines

☆ Cornflakes

☆ Minced chicken livers

☆ Worms with a luscious tomato and cheese sauce

Mmm, tasty!

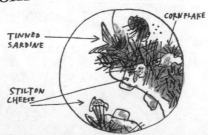

CORNFLAKE

TINNED SARDINE

STILTON CHEESE

☆ Snozzcumber sandwiches

☆ Frobscottle

An exotic delicacy that tastes of frogskins and rotten fish

☆ Chickens

☆ Geese

☆ Hams

☆ Bacon

☆ A jug of delicious cider

Answers on page 149

Cuckoo!

May is the month of the cuckoo, a bird of very nasty habits. Here are some cuckoo facts:

1. It really does say '*Cuck-koo!*' just like its name. With its loud call, this is a bird that's heard rather than seen.

2. Unlike most other birds, cuckoos do not pair up and stay together.

3. The cuckoo is a big strong bird, with a wide wingspread and a long tail.

4. No cuckoo has ever bothered to build its own nest or hatch or feed its young. The female cuckoo simply lays her egg in another egg-filled nest.

5. When the baby cuckoo hatches, it turfs out the other chicks from the nest.

6. 'I say that the cuckoo is the nastiest bird in the sky' – Roald Dahl.

Famous Pets

Roald Dahl once owned a Jack Russell called Chopper who loved to eat Smarties. Here are some more celebrities and their pets:

Jake Gyllenhaal
Atticus, the German shepherd dog

Drew Barrymore
Flossie, the Lab-Chow dog

Reese Witherspoon
Frank Sinatra, the bulldog

Angelina Jolie
Harry, the rat

Mary-Kate Olson
Luca, the Labrador

Paul McCartney
Martha, the sheepdog

George Clooney
Max, the pig

Paris Hilton
Tinkerbell, the chihuahua

Swimming lessons

In the month of May, the pool at Roald Dahl's school was refilled with water. But not heated. Still, he learnt to swim when he was nine years old (and probably had to, so that he didn't freeze to death!).

Famous Channel swimmers

1875

Matthew Webb became the first person ever to swim the English Channel. It took 21 hours and 45 minutes.

1926

Gertrude Ederle became the first woman to swim the Channel. She beat the existing men's record by two hours with a time of 14 hours and 31 minutes.

1972

Lynne Cox became the youngest person to swim the Channel, beating both the men's and women's records with a time of 9 hours and 57 minutes. She was just 15 years old.

True or false?

Roald Dahl was an RAF fighter pilot who carried out daring raids during the Second World War.

True

You can read all about his amazing adventures in *Going Solo*.

Flying machines

Here are some of the amazing
aircraft that Roald Dahl flew:

Hawker Hart
A plane with more oomph,
and deadly machine guns
on the wings.

Tiger Moth
Roald Dahl was so tall,
his head stuck out of
the cockpit.

Hurricane
Powerful, speedy, tricky
and so little room in the cockpit
that Roald Dahl's knees almost
touched his chin.

Gladiator
A plane that fired
bullets through its
spinning propeller!

June

June 20th. 1926.

St Peter's

Weston-super-mare.

Dear Mama

I thank you for the cricket ball and the choclate you sent me, it is exacly the kind I wanted. I r have Swum two lengths so far and have not tried any more but I could do more. I can very nearly dive propely now, I hit the bottom but I had my hands infront of me so I did not hurt my self infact I rather liked it; I have nearly swum the bredth under water. I am sending you my half term report

See page 108

See page 119

Love from

Roald.

The Queen's birthday again

Queen Elizabeth II has not one, but *two* birthdays. Her real birthday is 21 April, but she has an official birthday* sometime in June or May or September, depending on where you are in the world. In the UK, her official birthday is the second Saturday in June, in New Zealand it's the first Monday in June and in most of Australia it's the second Monday in June, while in Canada it's the Monday on or before 24 May. In Western Australia, it's celebrated on the last Monday of September or the first Monday of October. If the Queen organized her diary really well, she could go to six of her own birthday parties every year!

* This tradition began when Edward VII – the Queen's great-grandfather – decided that it was a bit dull having a birthday in November and that it would be much nicer to celebrate when the weather was warmer and sunnier. And he was king. So he did.

Royal Star

The Queen is one of the very few real people who have starred in one of Roald Dahl's books. Give yourself a right royal pat on the back if you remembered that this book was *The BFG*.

Monarchs

since the Norman Conquest in 1066 and the dates of their reigns.

House of Normandy

1066–1087 William I
1087–1100 William II
1100–1135 Henry I
1135–1154 Stephen

House of Plantagenet

1154–1189 Henry II
1189–1199 Richard I
1199–1216 John
1216–1272 Henry III
1272–1307 Edward I
1307–1327 Edward II
1327–1377 Edward III
1377–1399 Richard II

House of Lancaster

1399–1413 Henry IV
1413–1422 Henry V
1422–1461 Henry VI

House of York

1461–1483 Edward IV
1483 Edward V
1483–1485 Richard III

House of Tudor

1485–1509 Henry VII
1509–1547 Henry VIII
1547–1553 Edward VI
1553–1558 Mary I
1558–1603 Elizabeth I

House of Stuart

1603–1625 James I
1625–1649 Charles I

Period of Interregnum

1649–1653 Commonwealth/
protectorate

1653–1658 Protectorate of
Oliver Cromwell

1658–1659 Protectorate of
Richard Cromwell

House of Stuart restored

1660–1685 Charles II
1685–1688 James II
1689–1694 William III and
Mary II (jointly)

1694–1702 William III
(sole ruler)

1702–1714 Anne

House of Hanover

1714–1727 George I
1727–1760 George II
1760–1820 George III
1820–1830 George IV
1830–1837 William IV
1837–1901 Victoria

House of Saxe-Coburg-Gotha

1901–1910 Edward VII

House of Windsor

1910–1936 George V
(Saxe-Coburg-Gotha until 1917)
1936 Edward VIII
1936–1952 George VI
1952– Elizabeth II

Who ate what?

Roald Dahl loved food. His stories are sprinkled with tasty – and not so tasty – nibbles too. Can you match these familiar names with the meals they ate?

Answers on page 149

James Henry Trotter

Charlie Bucket

Bruce Bogtrotter

The BFG

Danny

A huge chocolate cake

Watery cabbage soup

Juicy peach flesh

Roasted pheasant

Eight eggs, twelve sausages, sixteen rashers of bacon and a heap of fried potatoes (for starters . . .)

The Roald Dahl Museum and Story Centre

Since June 2005, the museum in Great Missenden, Buckinghamshire, has welcomed Roald Dahl fans from around the world. Interactive films and displays tell the story of his life and works.

To find out more about the Roald Dahl Museum, visit its website: **roalddahlmuseum.org**

True or false?

The title of one of Roald Dahl's books makes more sense when read backwards than it does forwards.

True

When *Esio Trot* is read from back to front, it says *tortoise*!

Backwards
and forwards

A palindrome is a word, phrase or sentence that says exactly the same thing, whether you read it front to back or back to front. Check out this list and then see if you can think of your own . . .

MUM

DAD

NOON

RADAR

DON'T NOD

EVIL OLIVE

DR AWKWARD

KAYAK

MADAM, I'M ADAM

TOO HOT TO HOOT

WAS IT A CAT I SAW?

Exam time

Find out if you're a clever clogs
Matilda or just a Twit . . .

1. What did Matilda's wheeler-dealer dad do for a living?

2. Can you name James Henry Trotter's nasty aunts?

3. Did Roald Dahl like beards?

4. Who starred as Willy Wonka in the film version of *Charlie and the Chocolate Factory* (2005)?

5. Who were Farmer Boggis, Farmer Bunce and Farmer Bean?

6. How many Golden Tickets does Willy Wonka hide inside chocolate-bar wrappers?

7. What's the name of the little boy who tells the story of *The Witches*?

8. Which of the following grandparents did not belong to Charlie Bucket?
   a) Grandpa Joe
   b) Grandma Jolene
   c) Grandpa George
   d) Grandma Georgina

9. What do the initials BFG stand for?

10. What are tough and chewy and nasty and bitter?

Answers on page 149

Roald Dahl says...

'During this month the tadpoles in the ponds are beginning to sprout tiny arms and legs, and soon they will be turning into small frogs. Be nice to frogs, by the way. They are your friends in the garden. They eat the beastly slugs and never harm your flowers.'

Q: What's a frog's favourite drink?

A: *Croaka-Cola.*

Frog facts

1. There are around 5,000 different types of frogs worldwide.

2. Frogs have poisonous skin glands.

3. Female frogs lay between a few hundred and a few thousand eggs – they take just a few days to hatch.

4. Only male frogs croak. Some kinds of frogs inflate their throats to sound louder. They can inflate their throats so much that they're larger than their heads!

5. Small frogs live on average for just one year. Large frogs live longer.

6. The smallest frog in the world is the Gold Frog from Brazil. It's only 10mm long!

7. All frogs eat other animals, usually insects. None eat plants.

Wimbledon fortnight

The All England Lawn Tennis Club

hosts the Wimbledon Championships during the last week of June
and the first week of July every year. It's one of the four Grand
Slam tournaments (so called because they're very important)
held throughout the year. The others are the **Australian Open**
(Melbourne, January), the **French Open** (Paris, June) and the **US
Open** (New York City, September). If a tennis player or a doubles
team holds all four titles at the same time, they have achieved the
elusive **Grand Slam**. These players actually did it:

☆ **Martina Navratilova (1983–4)**

☆ **Steffi Graf (1988, 1993–4)**

☆ **Serena Williams (2002–3)**

July

St. Peter's
Weston-s-mare.

July 15ᵗʰ 1928.

Dear Mama
thanks for your letter. Its been fearfully hot the last few days, and so please excuse writing because, having been to church, we've had to change hastily an into 'cricket shirt only,' so my hand is rather shaky.
Last Wednesday we played the Parish church choir boys, with rather a flabby team, because we beat them so hollow last time.
Yesterday we had some swiming sports, the 4 lengths open, I won my heat, and hope to come 2ⁿᵈ on the final.
By the way, I'm coming home by the 12.25 not the 12.32, it arrives at Paddington at 4.5.
Love
Roald

See page 124

See page 108

The Ashes

This famous – but very tiny – trophy is said to contain a burnt bail. It symbolizes the ashes of English cricket after Australia defeated the English team in 1882. Ever since, the two countries have battled against each other in the Ashes Test Series. Australia has won more times (125 times compared to England's 96 wins), but in 2005, England sensationally snatched back the Ashes in a nail-biting 2–1 victory.

Cricket speak

Baggy green – the hat worn by Australian players, so called because it is baggy and green

Bails – the two tiny pieces of wood that sit precariously on top of the stumps

Crumble – how the pitch is described when it's especially rough and pitted

Duck – a score of zero

Follow on – when the batting team are made to bat again, as soon as they are bowled out

Googly – a delivery by a right-arm spin-bowler, which a right-handed batsman may think will spin one way, but in fact spins in the opposite direction

Grubber* – a ball that stays very low after bouncing

Jaffa – a ball that is bowled so well that it cannot be played

LBW – this stands for Leg Before Wicket, which means that the ball would have hit the stumps, were the player's leg not in front of them

Over – when six balls have been bowled

Stumps – the three upright wooden sticks at either end of the pitch

Yorker – a ball that whizzes under the bat near the batsman's toes. Curiously, it's also known as a Sandshoe Crusher.

*The Grubber was also the name of the sweet shop in
The Giraffe and the Pelly and Me.

School reports

Roald Dahl's school reports weren't always good, they weren't always bad, but they were always entertaining. Here's his report from 1930, when he was fourteen years old.

REPTON SCHOOL.
HALF TERM REPORT.

Christmas... Term, 1930

Form. Remove. C. Boy's Name... R. Dahl

Place for Half Term. 19

Number in Form. 22

English Subjects.		14	A persistent muddler, writing and saying the opposite of what he means. Fails to correct this by revision or thought. Has possibilities. *S.H.O.*
	Set	Place	
Latin. M. M-O.	3	16 17	Very weak, especially in Composition.
Greek Geography J. F. C.	–	–	Weak, but may improve.
German			
French.			
		19	Weak, for the same reasons as in English. *S.H.O.*
Mathematics.			
Science.			

Housemaster's Report. He probably finds his new form master a bit puzzling. But as long as he attends & tries, he will get on.

B.S. 25.

More school reports of the rich, famous and super-talented

'He will either become a millionaire or go to prison'

Richard Branson,
multi-millionaire
entrepreneur

'Hopeless.
Certainly on the
road to failure'

John Lennon, The Beatles

'A good science
student, but rather
mediocre in French'

Albert Einstein,
Nobel-prize-winning
physicist

'Does not
quite understand
the meaning of
hard work'

Sir Winston Churchill,
British Prime Minister
during the Second World War

'He makes
good cakes'

David Beckham,
world-famous
football player

Leaving school

In July 1934, Roald Dahl left school forever. Can you guess which of the following five jobs he *didn't* do?

1. **Shell Oil Company representative in East Africa**

2. **Best selling children's author**

3. **RAF fighter pilot**

4. **Doctor**

5. **Something incredibly secret for the British intelligence service**

Answer on page 149

Q: What did the pilot say as he left home to go to work?

A: *Must fly now!*

Now and then

These famous people didn't always do famous jobs.

	Now	Then
Harrison Ford	Actor	Carpenter
Brad Pitt	Actor	Delivering fridges
Jennifer Aniston	Actor	Waitress
Steven Spielberg	Director	Whitewashing fruit trees
Danny DeVito	Actor/Director	Hairdresser

True or false?

Roald Dahl rode a motorbike to school.

True

In his last summer term ever, Roald Dahl rode his beloved Ariel 500cc to a secret location near his school. (Motorbikes were quite forbidden – if he had been caught, he would have been expelled on the spot.) On Sunday afternoons, he would put on his disguise – waders, helmet, goggles and windproof jacket – and zoom around the countryside, right under the nose of his strict headteacher.

Roald Dahl's
top tips for becoming an author

1. You should have a lively imagination.

2. You should be able to write well. By that I mean you should be able to make a scene come alive in the reader's mind. Not everybody has this ability. It is a gift, and you either have it or you don't.

3. You must have stamina. In other words, you must be able to stick to what you are doing and never give up, for hour after hour, day after day, week after week and month after month.

4. You must be a perfectionist. That means you must never be satisfied with what you have written until you have rewritten it again and again, making it as good as you possibly can.

5. You must have strong self-discipline. You are working alone. No one is employing you. No one is around to give you the sack if you don't turn up for work, or to tick you off if you start slacking.

6. If helps a lot if you have a keen sense of humour. This is not essential when writing for grown-ups, but for children, it's vital.

7. You must have a degree of humility. The writer who thinks that his work is marvellous is heading for trouble.

The best and worst* bits of

Norway
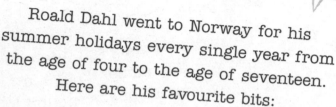

Roald Dahl went to Norway for his summer holidays every single year from the age of four to the age of seventeen. Here are his favourite bits:

1. **The celebration feast with his Norwegian relatives.**

2. **Krokaan** – crisp burnt toffee bits that were mixed with ice cream.

3. **The island of Tjöme** – the greatest place on Earth, according to Roald.

4. **The Hard Black Stinker** – a battered old motorboat that Mrs Dahl used to ferry her children around the fjords.

5. **Packing his ancient half-sister's boyfriend's pipe with goat's droppings instead of tobacco. The results were spectacular. (To find out more, read Boy.)**

*The worst bit was the sea journey from Newcastle to Oslo. Roald was horribly seasick all the way there. And all the way back.

Facts about Norway

Area:
385,199 sq km

Population:
4,617,000

Capital:
Oslo

Chief of State:
King Harald V

Biggest exports:
oil, natural gas and fish

Standard of living:
ranked number one in the world in 2005

Number of islands:
over 150,000

Most famous historical warrior inhabitants:
the Vikings (AD 800 to 1050)

Density of population:
15 people per square kilometre (in England, there are 359 people per square kilometre)

Daylight hours:
in northern Norway, the sun never sets between the middle of May and the middle of July. For two months in winter, it never rises.

Did you know?

A long-horned grasshopper doesn't have ears on the sides of its head. It has one on each side of its stomach. Weird? Then how about this: crickets' and katydids' ears are in their front legs, just below their knees.

Q: Where would you put an injured insect?

A: *An antambulance*

Q: What's a grasshopper's favourite game?

A: Cricket

August

A letter written by Roald in August 1934
– in the middle of the Atlantic Ocean!
He was seventeen.

R.M.S. NOVA SCOTIA.

Thursday   at sea.

Dear Mama

This is thursday & we are due in at St. Johns this afternoon at about 5 o'clock. We've had a marvellous voyage. Woke up on Saturday morning to find ourselves off the coast of Ireland. It looked a marvellous place. Later Scotland appeared on the other side & I took some photos of the Giants Causeway. After lunch, when we had left the coast of Ireland it started to blow & we didn't feel so good. However we remained on deck, and caught the wireless operator being sick over the side!

Globetrotting

At the beginning of August 1934, Roald Dahl went on his very first grown-up adventure. He and thirty other boys sailed to Newfoundland in Canada to take part in a back-packing expedition. Other marvellous and exotic places where Roald Dahl lived include:

☆ 1936–39 Dar es Salaam, Tanzania
☆ 1939–40 Nairobi, Kenya
☆ 1940 Habbaniya, Iraq
☆ 1940 Ismailia, Egypt
☆ 1940–41 Alexandria, Egypt
☆ 1941 Elevsis (near Athens), Greece
☆ 1941 Haifa, Israel
☆ 1942–45 Washington DC, USA
☆ 1948–60 New York City, USA
☆ 1960–90 Great Missenden, Buckinghamshire, England

Roald Dahl says...

'August is the month when baby adders are born in heathy, hilly places, and baby grass snakes emerge from their eggs in rotting leaves and old compost heaps.'

True or false?

Pemmican is mouth-watering Norwegian ice cream. Roald Dahl ate it non-stop during his summer holidays.

False

It's actually a high-protein snack made from pulverized meat, dried berries and fat. It's packed with energy, which makes it ideal for tough journeys, such as the long trek Roald Dahl once made through Newfoundland. Unfortunately, pemmican isn't as delicious as ice cream.

The **10** weirdest ice-cream flavours

**Bored with vanilla, strawberry and chocolate?
Why not try these?**

Bacon and eggs

Avocado

Chilli

Cow tongue

Wasabi
(A type of
horseradish)

Eel

Shrimp

Horseflesh

Sardines
on toast

Octopus

(These flavours are real, not made-up – honest!)

'First, the butterfly lays its eggs. It lays them in vast quantities, usually between two and three hundred, but very few of these eggs survive. They are food for countless animals, birds, mice, lizards, spiders and many insects.

Second, the surviving eggs hatch into larvae or caterpillars. These caterpillars gorge themselves on leaves in preparation for the next stage.

Third, the caterpillars turn into pupae or chrysalises, which hibernate through the winter and emerge again as butterflies.'

Star spotting

The seven brightest stars are also known as the Big Dipper or the Plough.

August is a splendid month to look out for stars in clear summer skies. And if you're lucky enough to be in the countryside, or on holiday somewhere remote, then they'll be even brighter. Here are some of the most famous constellations (a group of stars) in the northern hemisphere at this time of year:

Ursa Major

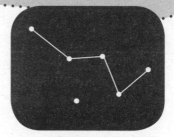

Cassiopeia

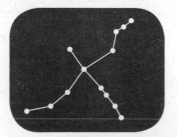

Cygnus

Draco

The North Star

Also called the Pole Star or Polaris, the North Star is the most famous star in the northern sky. It stays in the same place while all the other stars circle round it, so, for thousands of years, people have used it to help them find their way across sea and land (very handy if you get lost). You can always tell which way is north by looking at the North Star. If you stood at the North Pole, the North Star would be directly overhead.

To find the North Star in the sky, first find the Big Dipper and follow the two stars at the end of the basin upwards. This should lead you directly to the North Star.

Bored with the Summer holidays?

Then learn Morse code and read the secret message below. (Each word is in brackets and there's a forward slash at the end of every letter.)

Morse code was used to send the first telegraph messages in the 1830s, before the telephone had been invented. The code is still used by radio amateurs around the world. The most famous Morse code message is the emergency signal **S-O-S**.

(._/_._/_._/_._/_ _ _/._/_ _/._/._/_ _/_ _ _.) (_ /_ _ _ _)

(._/_ _ _/._/_._/_._/._ ..) (_ ..I._/._..././_ _./._ _./._ _ _ _ _.)(_ /.._../ .)

(_ _/_ _ _/._../.._) (_ /._../._/_ ./._/._ ./._../._ _I._/ _ ./_ _ _.)

(_ _/ _ _ _/_ _ ./.I_ ./) (.._/_ .) (...../..I._/...)

(._ _/._../_ _ _/._ ../._ ..I.) (._ ../.I../.. _ ./.)

(._ _ ./._I...) (_ .../././.I._ ./._ _ _.) (_ .../_ _ _ I._ ./._ /_.)

Answers on page 149

142

A	B	C	D	E
._	_...	_._.	_..	.

F	G	H	I	J
.._.	__.	....	..	.___

K	L	M	N	O
_._	._..	__	_.	___

P	Q	R	S	T
.__.	__._	._.	...	_

U	V	W	X	Y
.._	..._	.__	_.._	_.__

Z	.	?	-	,
__..	._._._	..__..	_..._	_._._.

Did you know?

The true inventor of the Morse code as we know it today was not Mr Morse, but his partner, Alfred Vail. Samuel Morse invented the original equipment and code for the electric telegraph, but the system had problems. Vail, who had agreed to build the system's hardware, was forced to create a completely new printing mechanism and a new code to make it work. This was the dashes and dots 'Morse' code which has been used ever since.

Q: What's yellow, fuzzy, and goes at 180 miles per hour?

A: A fuel-injected peach.

Q: What's very very tall and goes 'tnaig drawkcab a'?

A: A giant talking backwards

Last words

Throughout his long life, Roald Dahl lived by this inspiring verse, which was written in 1920 by US poet, Edna St Vincent Millay:

My candle burns at both ends

It will not last the night;

But ah, my foes, and oh, my friends —

It gives a lovely light.

More marvellous Roald Dahl reads

THE BFG (1982)

BOY:TALES OF CHILDHOOD (1984)

BOY and GOING SOLO (1992)

CHARLIE AND THE CHOCOLATE FACTORY (1964)

CHARLIE AND THE GREAT GLASS ELEVATOR (1973)

THE COMPLETE ADVENTURES OF CHARLIE AND MR WONKA (1987)

DANNY THE CHAMPION OF THE WORLD (1975)

GEORGE'S MARVELLOUS MEDICINE (1981)

GOING SOLO (1986)

JAMES AND THE GIANT PEACH (1961)

MATILDA (1988)

THE WITCHES (1983)

Teenage fiction

THE GREAT AUTOMATIC GRAMMATICZATOR AND OTHER STORIES (1996)

SKIN AND OTHER STORIES (2000)

THE VICAR OF NIBBLESWICKE (1991)

THE WONDERFUL STORY OF HENRY SUGAR AND SIX MORE (1977)

For younger readers

THE ENORMOUS CROCODILE (1978)

ESIO TROT (1990)

FANTASTIC MR FOX (1970)

THE GIRAFFE AND THE PELLY AND ME (1985)

THE MAGIC FINGER (1966)

THE TWITS (1980)

Picture books

DIRTY BEASTS with Quentin Blake (1983)

THE ENORMOUS CROCODILE with Quentin Blake (1978)

THE GIRAFFE AND THE PELLY AND ME
with Quentin Blake (1985)

THE MINPINS with Patrick Benson (1991)

REVOLTING RHYMES with Quentin Blake (1982)

Answers

The great conker quiz page 16

1. c) Less dedicated players may use methods a) and b) to harden their conkers, but nothing beats patience and a dry place. After a year, your conker will be rock hard and very formidable. 2. a) Always choose a flat, sharp-edged conker. 3. Absolutely, most definitely b). 4. What? You have no idea? Check out Roald Dahl's book, *Boy*. It was, of course, Conker 109, which was eventually smashed by Perkins's Conker 74 in an epic conker contest. Everybody knows that.

The scrambled fireworks page 33

Roman candle, crack banger, fire serpent, rocket, golden rain.

New Year's resolutions page 56

1. Willy Wonka – it was never the same after the Great Glass Elevator made a quick exit ... 2. Matilda. 3. James Henry Trotter. 4. Charlie Bucket. 5. Mr Twit – well, you'd do the same if you'd accidentally eaten worms, wouldn't you?

All over the world page 83

1. *Charlie and the Chocolate Factory*. 2. *The BFG*. 3. *Danny the Champion of the World*. 4. *The Magic Finger*. 5. *The Twits*. 6. *George's Marvellous Medicine*. 7. *Esio Trot*. 8. *The BFG*. 9. *Charlie and the Great Glass Elevator*. 10. *The Twits*. 11. *The Giraffe and the Pelly and Me*.

Whose lunchbox? pages 104–105

The Twits, the BFG, Fantastic Mr Fox.

'Who ate what?' page 116

James Henry Trotter: juicy peach flesh. Charlie Bucket: watery cabbage soup. Bruce Bogtrotter: a huge chocolate cake. The BFG: eight eggs, twelve sausages, sixteen rashers of bacon and a heap of fried potatoes (for starters …). Danny: roasted pheasant.

Exam time page 119

1. He was a car dealer – and a rather dodgy one at that. 2. Aunt Spiker and Aunt Sponge. 3. Absolutely not. He *hated* hairy faces. If you don't believe me, read *The Twits*. 4. Johnny Depp. 5. They were the farmers who tried to outwit *Fantastic Mr Fox*. 6. Five. 7. Goodness knows! You can read *The Witches* from start to finish and back again, but you'll never find the answer. 8. b) Grandma Jolene, of course. Charlie's real grandmother was Grandma Josephine. 9. Big Friendly Giant. 10. Children. Or so says the Notsobig One in *The Enormous Crocodile*.

Leaving school page 128

4. Roald Dahl was never a doctor, although he secretly longed to be one. He did, however, help to invent a tiny medical valve for draining excess – and dangerous – fluid from the brains of sick children.

Morse code message page 142

According to Roald Dahl, the most thrilling moment in his whole life was being born.

Charlie and the Chocolate Factory

Roald Dahl found *Charlie and the Chocolate Factory* one of the most difficult books to write. His first draft of the story included fifteen horrible children. His nephew Nicholas read it and said it was rotten and boring, so Roald Dahl realized he needed to rewrite it!

The idea for Charlie came from Roald Dahl's schooldays, when he and other classmates were occasionally asked by Cadbury's to test newly invented chocolate bars. He used to dream of inventing his own famous chocolate bar that would win the praise of Mr Cadbury himself.

The Twits

Roald Dahl kept an old school exercise book in which he wrote all the ideas for his stories. Some of the ideas stayed in there for twenty or more years before he came to incorporate them into books. The idea for *The Twits* simply said 'do something against beards'. Roald Dahl was not a fan of beards and said he never understood why a man wanted to hide his face behind a big bushy beard.

Danny the Champion of the World

Danny the Champion of the World is one of Roald Dahl's only books that is based on first-hand experience. When he moved to Buckinghamshire, he became friends with a man called Claude who worked in the local butcher's. Claude had a passion for poaching and the two of them would sometimes sneak into the local woods in the dead of night to catch pheasants. Roald Dahl never caught a single bird, but enjoyed the thrill of the experience. Like Danny, Roald's own children learned to drive at a very young age. He taught his daughter Ophelia to drive when she was only ten years old! The caravan in this story is based on the sky-blue caravan that sits in Roald Dahl's garden.

The BFG

Roald Dahl invented the story of the BFG for his own children. He would sometimes put a ladder up to their window when they were in bed and stir the curtains or even push through a bamboo cane as if the BFG himself were really outside blowing dreams into their bedroom. The BFG's friend, Sophie, is named after a real Sophie, Roald's granddaughter. She is the only family member whose name he used for a character in one of his books. Of all the characters he created, the BFG was probably his favourite, as he valued kindness above all other qualities in life.

Matilda

Roald Dahl remembered what it was like to live in a child's world and kept this in mind when he wrote *Matilda*. He once said that in order to see life from a child's point of view you had to get down on your hands and knees and look up at the adults towering above you, telling you what to do. Matilda's triumph over the nasty adults in her life is based on this theory.

George's Marvellous Medicine

Roald Dahl had a little brown and white Jack Russell terrier called Chopper. Little did anyone think he'd be inspired to write Chopper's bottom into this book!

Roald Dahl wrote all his children's books from a specially built writing hut in the apple orchard of his house in Great Missenden. It was so private that he never let anyone in to clean it and it gathered dust for more than fifteen years! It was full of litter and spiders' webs – he adored spiders.

The Witches

Just like the grandmother in this story, Roald Dahl's parents were Norwegian. He spent many happy holidays in Norway and much of the Norwegian details in the book are taken from his childhood experiences. The grandmother is actually based on his own mother.

Roald Dahl's children had fifty different-coloured glass balls hanging from their bedroom ceiling. Their father told them that they were witch balls and if any witch came near in the night she would flee in fright at her ghastly reflection in the balls.

James and the Giant Peach

James and the Giant Peach was Roald Dahl's second book for children. He wrote it in New York in the winter of 1960 after a stretch of seventeen years in which he had written only short stories for adults. Roald Dahl's baby son, Theo, had a terrible accident while Roald was writing this book, and he said that being able to disappear into this fantasy world for a few hours each day helped him through the crisis. Today, happily, both Theo and James are very much alive and well.

THE
ROALD DAHL
FOUNDATION

Providing practical support for children with
brain, blood and literacy problems

What is the Roald Dahl Foundation?

As well as being a great storyteller, Roald Dahl was also a man who gave generously of his time and money to help people in need, especially children. After he died in 1990, his widow, Felicity, set up the Roald Dahl Foundation to continue this generous tradition. Its support spreads far and wide. Since it began, the Foundation has given over £4 million across the UK.

The Foundation aims to help children and young people in practical ways and in three areas that were particularly important to Roald Dahl during his lifetime: neurology, haematology and literacy. It makes grants to hospitals and charities, as well as to individual children and their families.

Supporting the Roald Dahl Foundation

Funded partly through the Foundation's original endowment, it
also benefits from a range of fundraising, most notably the national
sponsored reading event in Readathon.® The Foundation
also benefits from an ambitious programme of new
orchestral music for children based on Roald
Dahl's stories and rhymes, specially
commissioned on its behalf.

To find out more about the Roald Dahl Foundation
or to make an online donation visit the website at
www.roalddahlfoundation.org

The Roald Dahl Foundation is a
registered charity, no. 1004230

Take a tour of Roald Dahl's scrumdiddlyumptious official website with your favourite characters at www.roalddahl.com